"I can do tricks, too!" Rupert told his friends. "If you can help me build a ramp, I'll show you!"

Soon the friends were busily building.

When they were finished, Rupert backed up on his scooter, then whizzed over the ramp.

Everyone cheered.

As soon as Rupert landed, he wanted to go again – even faster!

"That's not possible," said Bill, checking his electronic book of facts.

"Oh yes it is," said Ping Pong. "I know just the spell!"

"I don't think magic and scooters are a good idea," said Edward, anxiously. But the others were too excited to listen.

Ping Pong began to chant:

"Scooter with your force
Go faster of course
So gallop and canter
Like a wild, wild horse!"

"A horse?" echoed Edward in alarm. But Ping Pong had already sprinkled her magic dust.

Whoa!" cried Rupert. The scooter had suddenly bucked underneath him, as if it was trying to get away.

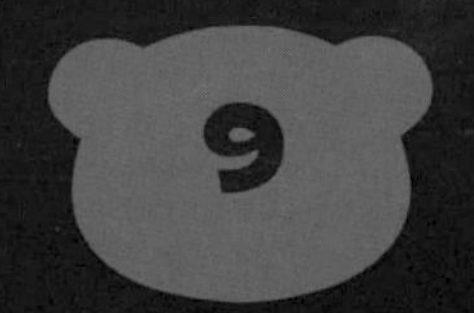

"Woo hoo!" cried Rupert as he soared off the end of the ramp.

But his excitement changed to alarm when the scooter started trying to shake him off in mid-air!

Panicking, Ping Pong threw some magic dust into the air. When it touched the scooter, the handlebars disappeared, and it turned into a skateboard!

Rupert's skateboard landed, but it was going so fast that it whizzed straight back up the ramp, and Rupert was thrown into the air again!

"Scooting skateboard stop stop STOP!" Ping Pong shouted desperately. But that only made the skateboard freeze in mid-air, then drop like a stone.

"Argh! shouted Rupert. "Help!"

All the noise had brought Raggety out of the trees.

"Do something!" Edward called to him.

Raggety thought fast. "Leaping leaves, leapetty leap!" he cried.

Hundreds of leaves fluttered from the tree, piling up to give Rupert a soft landing.

"Please, thank you," said Raggety to the leaves.

Everyone was relieved to find Rupert was all right. But when they looked around, they saw the skateboard trundling off into the forest on its own.

"We'll have to track it like a wild animal!" said Bill, pulling out a magnifying glass. "Let's go and search for footprints."

"Tyre marks!" corrected Rupert.

They soon ran into a problem. The tyre tracks all went in different directions! So they had to split up.

Ping Pong and Ming went into the forest.

"We'll never find anything in all these trees!" cried Ping Pong in frustration.

So she chanted a spell . . . and disappeared! She'd spelled herself up a tree by mistake.

Rupert and Bill had a bit more luck. They managed to creep up on the skateboard as it rested in a quiet glade.

While they watched, its shape blurred . . . and then it was a scooter again.

"Psst!" whispered Rupert to Bill. They were hiding behind the trees, watching. "It's turning back to normal!"

"Let's use those ivy tendrils as lassoes," whispered Rupert to Bill.

The friends twirled the ivy lassoes and flung them hard at the scooter. But things did not go to plan.

Rupert's lasso caught Bill, and Bill's caught Rupert. The scooter rocked backwards and forward, then whizzed off. It was definitely laughing at them!

The scooter raced on at top speed. It passed Edward and Raggety, knocking them into a heap! Then it sped around the outside of Ping Pong's Pagoda.

"Look!" cried Ping Pong, coming down the path. "We'll get it this time, Ming!"

Ming chased the scooter, yapping frantically. But it simply turned around and zoomed off.

But the scooter couldn't run forever! As it came out on to the green, Rupert and Bill ran up to it from one side, and all their friends from the other. The scooter tried to back away.

"Ssh, don't scare it," whispered Rupert.

"Yes," agreed Bill. "We must be quiet and move slowly."

"Ping Pong," Rupert whispered. "Change the spell!"

"Oh no," said Bill. "Not more magic! I'll look in my book."

"We have to do something!" protested Rupert. Looking slightly worried, Ping Pong began to chant.

Then, to everyone's relief, the scooter fell over with a thump. The spell had worked!

Rupert's scooter was normal again. He climbed back on, and whizzed off across the green.

His front wheel rose into the air – but it wasn't magic controlling the scooter now!

"WheeeeEEEEE!"

The End

First published in Great Britain in 2007
by Egmont UK Limited
239 Kensington High Street, London W8 6SA

ISBN 978 1 4052 3197 8
1 3 5 7 9 10 8 6 4 2
Printed in China